A CHRISTMAS BABY TO HEAL HIS HEART

AMISH CHRISTMAS ROMANCE

SARAH MILLER

CHAPTER ONE

The birds in the distance chirped a song that created a relaxing atmosphere in the sitting room. Katie Mueller peered through the window, reminiscing on the life she had just a few months earlier. With a sigh, she straightened her apron as she leaned onto the windowsill and tried to concentrate on the bird song.

It was her first spring as a married woman and she was not as happy about it as she should have been. She had always believed that a couple should fall in love before marriage. But when she was unable to make a match, out of necessity that *was nee* longer the way she looked at marriage. Instead, she tried to focus on the love that came from companionship.

After all, her parents had an arranged marriage and they loved each other deeply. So, love wasn't necessary at the start, was it?

At the end of the last summer, her parents persuaded her that an arranged marriage was the best thing for her. They were worried about her, wanting her to settle down before it was too late. And luckily, a match was found in Levi. He had just moved to Faith's Creek after living in Ohio and had decided to take on reviving a farm that had long been neglected by the previous owner, one who had been too ill to take care of it. Bishop Amos Beiler and his *fraa* Sarah convinced him that a *fraa* would help him with the running of the farm. When the two were introduced everyone saw an immediate match and over time the couple started to see it too.

Katie sighed and closed her eyes for a few seconds as she remembered the wedding. It was beautiful and everyone wished them the happiest of marriage. But it wasn't happy. *Jah*, they were civil to each other, but they were far from feeling love. They were ideal companions, just nothing more.

Sadness washed over her and her eyes welled up with a thin layer of tears that blurred her vision. The dream of having a husband who would open his heart to her was still alive inside her. If that happened she knew she would do the same and they could have the love that existed between her parents. But that was impossible now, wasn't it? Levi wasn't open to being anything other than what they were. And being friends who shared the same last name was never going to be enough for her. She deserved a *familye* of her own. She deserved to feel a *boppli* in her belly and know the love of her husband without him having to say the words.

"Do you want anything to drink?"

Katie wiped her eyes with the back of her hand and turned around with smiling lips to greet Abigail, her sister.

"I had something earlier."

"Why do you look so sad?"

Katie shrugged her shoulders. Abigail had always been an intuitive one. "Some things in life are just not what you expected them to be."

"And that made you sad," Abigail asked with raised eyebrows.

"Why did it take you so long to get here, little sister?" Katie asked.

"Jeremiah was showing me the *haus* he wants us to move into," she said. "His parents are planning to give him a plot of land right after the marriage and there is a small *haus* already on it."

"Do you like it?" Katie asked, raising her eyebrow. Her sister wasn't very picky but she had been dreaming about marrying her first love for a very long time and that dream included everything up to the number of *kinner* they would have and the way their *haus* would look.

"*Jah.* It needs some work but it is perfect for us since it will just be the two of us... for now. We can always expand when that changes."

The passion in Abigail's eyes made Katie remember the shortcomings in her own marriage. But it also made her really happy for her sister. She got up from the window seat and walked over to her, engulfing her in her arms and squeezing her gently.

"I know you will have a wonderful life with him," she whispered.

When she released Abigail, the younger girl was beaming with pride and happy expectations. At eighteen, Abigail had found the love of her life, who was the same age as her and he had asked her to marry him. The wedding was in a few days and her brown eyes were brimming with the joy she felt, the joy Katie hoped she would have throughout her marriage and for the rest of her life. Seeing her happy made Katie less worried about her own situation. Maybe everyone wasn't expected to find the love she dreamed of. But she was happy that her sister had found it.

The sisters sat beside each other on the window seat and looked out to the garden they grew up tending to. Soon, neither of them would live in their parent's *haus* but they still had the happy memories of their childhood to look back on.

"Are you nervous?" Katie asked.

"*Nee.* Jeremiah is my childhood friend and confidant. My best friend. Marrying him feels like the right thing to do."

"*Gut.*" That was what Katie had wanted for herself so she was happy that her sister had found it. "I wish you nothing but the best. I want you to have the happiest life *Gott* can provide and live the dreams of *familye* you have always had."

"Thanks, Katie."

"Did *mamm* talk to you about the reception buffet yet?"

"*Jah,* she did. Don't worry some of your favorites are on it," she teased.

"I was not worried," Katie said with a chuckle. "I will be helping to make them anyway, so I will have a lot of chances to sample a few before the big event."

"Can you grab me some too?"

"Not too many, you won't get in that new dress you made." Katie smiled and laughed to let her sister know this was a joke.

"I think I will be too nervous to eat after the wedding. Save me a plate too, I will be starving when everyone leaves."

"Okay, I will save you a plate."

"*Denke*! You are the best sister in the world."

"I am your only sister."

They sat there for a few minutes more, talking about the wedding and the changes that would come after. It was late afternoon when Katie left her *familye haus* for her own, where she lived with her husband.

As soon as she got home she cleaned up and headed to the kitchen. Although they didn't love each other, they had both fallen into dutiful roles which saw him working mostly in the fields. She would take care of the *haus* and prepare meals. But she would also tend to the small animals and help in the fields in any way she could.

The mashed potatoes and chicken stew were done by the time he finished for the day. As Levi pushed the kitchen door opened, Katie placed the serving bowls on the table and turned toward him.

"You are right on time," she said.

"Great, I will get cleaned up and return."

Levi was older than she was but one could not tell from the way his red hair and green eyes made him appear youthful. He smiled at her before he disappeared out of the room and she remembered what she had thought when she had first laid eyes on him. At twenty-seven, he was a fine Amish *mann* and the prospect of marrying him had filled her with a lot of hope. But as they got to know each other, that hope faded, and now that they were married there was not much else she could do.

When Levi returned he sat down at the table and Katie joined him, watching as he shared a serving and then doing the same.

"This is good. *Denke*," he said after the first bite. But he didn't even look up at her.

As was usual, they ate in silence. As she chewed Katie watched her husband. Was this really the life she deserved? They were not childhood friends. Even after the marriage, they were hardly friends because she didn't know everything about him.

What could be different about her marriage? What could change? But the answer was *nee* more favorable than the reality she was living. She felt as if she was destined to be in a dull marriage for the rest of her life. And as much as she didn't want that there was nothing she could do about it. The Amish didn't believe in divorce and she was Amish.

CHAPTER TWO

*L*evi looked at the field of corn with admiration in his eyes. He had cared for it as it grew from seeds to knee-length stalks that were green with health. His lips curved into a satisfied smile as he examined a row closely to see if any weeds were lurking below them. Satisfied that they were okay, he moved on to the next set of crops.

Faith's Creek was more than he expected. It had been hard for him to start over because the idea had scared him. What if he had a worse life here than he had been living before? What if his destiny was to stay in Ohio? The fear was crippling, but he pushed through it by leaning on *Gott*. Through prayer, he realized that he deserved a second chance and through the help of Bishop Amos Beiler and his *fraa* Sarah, he now found that the best place for him to be was Faith's Creek. The best thing he could do was get a plot of land and focus his energy on the farm. With that plan in mind and *Gott's* blessing he also agreed to take a *fraa*.

He nodded as he remembered the checklist he had gone through before agreeing to wed Katie. He wanted a *fraa* who could care for the *haus*, who could help with harvesting and planting on the farm. When there were farmhands around she could host for them, making refreshments and food. She could help him handle some of the daily tasks on the farm and he would have someone to talk out decisions with, to discuss new crops, and make use of the ones they already grew. *Jah*, getting married was a *gut* idea.

"*Gut* day, Levi."

The voice startled him a little and he turned around to see Jeremiah Stoltz walking towards him.

"*Gut* morning, Jeremiah."

The other *mann* was younger than him, but at only eighteen years old he was about the same height as

Levi. His blue eyes were still shining with the lack of experience that came with youth and he pushed back his blond hair nervously beneath his straw hat.

"We will be *bruder*s-in-law soon," Jeremiah said. "I am excited about that. I can't wait to get married so that I can create what you have. The farm is amazing."

"*Denke*." Levi's lips curved into a smile and his heart beat faster with pride at his accomplishment. He looked around the farm, as far as his eyes could see, and Jeremiah walked forward to stand beside him and do the same.

"I can't believe your farm looks like this now. I remember walking past it when I was younger and going to school and wondering why it had not been flourishing. This is what I want my farm to look like."

"Your farm?" Levi asked, turning toward Jeremiah, with raised eyebrows. "You don't plan to keep working at the farm store?"

"*Nee*," he replied with a chuckle. "My parents are about to gift me my own plot of land. It is for Abigail and me to live on after our wedding. I am excited about it, but I am also a little worried."

"Why? You already know everything there is to know about farming."

"*Jah*. But I have never had my own farm before. It all feels like too much. I am not sure if I can run it on my own."

Levi looked at the other *mann* with searching eyes. He didn't meet his eyes, but he could tell that he was working his way up to asking for help.

"Are you saying such warm words about my farm because you want me to help you with yours?" Levi asked.

Embarrassed blue eyes stared back at Levi and Jeremiah started pushing back his hair again, still nervous.

"I... I would appreciate it. Anything you can help with or advise me on. I don't want to fail at my first harvest. Especially since I will have a *fraa* to take care of."

A sigh escaped Levi's lips and he turned away to examine the expanse of his farm. He had come a long way indeed. But it took a lot of hard work and most of it was because he had others to help him. There was just too much to do and he didn't have the time.

"I am sorry, Jeremiah," he grumbled. It was almost a whisper, but Jeremiah heard because his eyes turned sad and his shoulders slumped. "I have too much to do here to add any more work to my plate." He shook his head.

"Okay. I understand." Jeremiah's voice was low too and he sounded very disappointed, but Levi knew that he did understand. "I will leave you to your work now."

Levi watched as the young *mann* walked away slowly, his shoulders still slumped in defeat. He fiddled with the hoe in his hand as he watched him. He had been a young farmer once. He had *nee* idea what he was doing and it was a lot of pressure knowing that he had to have a successful harvest to be able to provide for himself for the rest of the year. Some people had helped him and he appreciated them for it. Without them, he had *nee* idea what would have happened or how long it would have taken him to learn all the lessons that shaped him as a farmer.

"Jeremiah," feeling suddenly ashamed, he called to the other man.

Jeremiah stopped and turned around, walking back to stand before Levi.

"I will help you whenever I can find the time. But only after you and Abigail are married."

"*Denke!*" Jeremiah's eyes lit up with happiness and his slump disappeared. "You do not know how much this means to me," he added, his voice laced with appreciation. "*Denke.* I am sure Abigail will be happy with the news. I will tell her now."

"Okay, I will see you around."

When he was alone again, Levi turned his attention back to the field he was tending before he was interrupted. But before he could get started again he noticed Katie by the hen *haus* collecting eggs. She had a half-filled basket in her hand and a look of determination on her face. They had gotten a few new hens and one, in particular, was more aggressive than the rest. Katie had complained about it a few times, wanting them to get rid of it so that she could collect eggs without it causing her trouble, but she seemed to be managing better lately.

She turned around and their eyes met, though it was from quite a distance. Her lips curved into a smile that reached her eyes and she waved at him. Levi nodded his head in acknowledgment, but he didn't raise his hand in reply. She stared at him for a moment and he got the feeling that she was upset with him, but then she went back into the hen *haus* and he went back to the field. There was a lot to get done and he didn't have time to dwell on things that may or may not affect him.

CHAPTER THREE

The barn was decorated in the most beautiful flowers that could be found in the county. Abigail and Jeremiah looked the happiest she had ever seen them as they stood before Bishop Beiler. He took them aside to talk to them privately, a tradition to make sure the couple was ready to get married before *Gott*. When that was done they returned to the front of the room, completed their vows and then hymns were sung to mark the special occasion.

Abigail turned to look at her *familye* and Katie smiled at her. She could tell that she was nervous but they had spoken about the marriage over a hundred times so she knew that Abigail wanted to get married.

When Amos announced that they were married, a murmur of congratulations went around the barn and everyone started to gather to congratulate the young couple. Katie felt her heart flood with joy as she watched them. Abigail deserved to be happy and she was glad that she was there to see her joined with the *mann* she had always loved... and a *mann* who loved her just the same. Quickly, she swallowed the lump in her throat, she would not spoil this day.

The meal was to be in two of the biggest rooms in their haus. Before everyone made their way over, Katie went across and started setting the food on the serving tables. She and her *mamm* had been preparing some of the food from the night before with the help of Jeremiah's *familye*. They had a lot of tables and chairs set up for the guests as well as enough room for them to walk around and talk to each other and greet the newly married couple. Their *mamm*, Susannah, and Katie were busy preparing the last of the food so that they could set them on the serving table.

"Is the salad ready?"

Katie whirled around and smiled at her *mamm*, Susannah Raber. She was in her forties but she had a much younger spirit. Her eyes were bright with the excitement of the day and her lips were curved into a smile. She was always a happy woman so Katie would not have expected her to be any different.

"*Jah*, I just finished it and put it out on the table."

"Great. I will pack the cupcakes onto a tray."

"You know they are likely to start having *kinner* before the year is out, right?" Susannah said happily, her voice a whisper, but her hope laced in every word.

"That would be a huge blessing," Katie said as she placed the stuff for making tea on a tray.

"When are you and Levi likely to be blessed in the same way?"

Katie's hands shook and the sugar spilled. Focusing on cleaning it up, Katie fumbled with the cleaning cloth, pausing to stare at her *mamm*, unsure how to respond.

"We..."

"Do you have any more fried chicken?"

Katie released a low sigh of relief when her *daed* popped into the kitchen.

"I will get you some," she said, rushing to the oven that was across the room.

He was not a very tall man, but his presence always commanded respect and his voice was always authoritative, though respectful, except when he was talking to his *fraa*. Susannah always joked about how different they were, yet they seemed to match perfectly. They raised two girls who were now both married and living with their husbands and they still carried on their own business and volunteered in the community whenever they could.

"How is Abigail holding up with everyone wanting to wish them happiness all at once?" Katie asked as she handed her father the tray laden with fried chicken.

"They are finally seated, but you know how Faith's Creek gets when there is a wedding. They will not get a break anytime soon."

James left and Susannah soon trailed after him with

more food for the serving table. When Katie finally got a chance to peek out at the reception she saw her sister surrounded by their *familye* and close friends, all laughing together and *nee d*oubt making her blush.

Since everything was under control, she slipped away and headed for the nearby meadow where she often went while she was growing up to get some time alone to think. It was a short walk, but the path was not as worn as it was when she had lived in her *familye haus*. She made her way to the flat top rock she always used to sit on and sat down, staring out at the meadow. All the animals were out, some feasting and the others resting, and she heard the birds chirping in the distance.

How was she supposed to tell her *mamm* that her marriage was in name only? How was she supposed to tell her that they had not even consummated the marriage even though it had been months?

Glancing up at the sky she realized how clear it was, there was not a cloud in sight. And she wondered why her mind wasn't the same. Why did she have to worry about telling her *mamm* the true nature of her marriage? Why wasn't there any love in her marriage?

Her eyes closed under the weight of her aching heart and she prayed.

"*Gott,* please show me how Levi and I can grow closer. I do not like the way we are now. This was never what I wanted from marriage and I find myself regretting it on some days. But I know that I am in this situation only by your will. What do you want me to do?"

The birds stopped and the wind seemed to still, but nothing else happened. If there was a sign, she didn't see it. Katie felt hopeless as she sat there. Levi was not a bad man. She had never seen him do anything that would cause her to fear or mistrust him. But he didn't have any inclination to change the nature of their relationship and she couldn't do it alone. She didn't even know where to start.

Her shoulder slumped as she made her way back to the reception. Maybe her marriage was as it was supposed to be. Maybe there was nothing she could do but suffer through it, knowing that she would never have the love she always dreamed of. She found an empty chair and sat down. As she watched everyone enjoy the reception she felt the desire to have a marriage filled with love grow stronger inside her. There was *nee* way she could spend the rest of her life with Levi in exactly the same way as she did right now. He was civil and he never did anything to hurt her. But he hardly ever showed any compassion so she wondered if he was even capable of falling in love.

Did she get married to the one person who was incapable of loving her? Surely that was not so. *Gott* gave everyone the capacity to love and so he could love, he just had to desire it.

"I will set aside two afternoons each week."

She turned when she heard Levi's voice and saw him speaking with Jeremiah while Abigail stood by with a warm smile trained on her husband. Katie was surprised. Levi had never taken so much time off from his own farm before. What was he planning?

"*Denke*, Levi," Jeremiah said. "It will help me a lot. You have the experience of running a farm and I am sure with your help I will be able to learn everything I need to know in *nee* time."

Farming.

A smile curved Katie's lips as she looked at the group, not sure if she should join them. At that moment she knew that there *was* kindness in Levi's distant heart and it gave her hope. She had never seen him make such a sacrifice before and it brought tears to her eyes as she thought about it. Her heart blossomed with hope for their future and her mind started to turn. There must be a way for her to get close to him and she would figure it out *nee* matter what.

CHAPTER FOUR

*L*evi ate his supper in silence and Katie watched him, wondering if it was the right time to ask. Her hands shook and she shoved some of the food into her mouth to hide it, hoping that he didn't see. He had cleared his afternoon so that he could help Jeremiah on his farm and she had finally devised a plan that would help them get closer. But for it to work, she needed him to take her with him.

"I have not seen Abigail in a while," she said, watching him closely, but pretending not to. "We do not see each other much these days. I am always busy here and she is trying to learn how to keep a home."

Levi looked up then and their eyes met. His green eyes were curious, but he didn't say anything. After a few seconds, he returned to his food and Katie released a slow sigh.

"Maybe I could go with you to their *haus*. That way I can catch up with Abigail while you work."

As the last morsel of food disappeared from his plate he looked up at her again, chewing slowly, his eyes squinting a little before relaxing.

"Sure. That seems like the best time since I will have already tended to everything on the farm before I go and I may stay there until supper, depending on the amount of work to be done."

"Great!" she beamed.

She could feel Levi's eyes on her as she scurried to get the dishes done and then pack a basket to take with her to Abigail's *haus*. This had to work, right? The more time they spent together, the more likely it was that some sort of connection would be formed between them. And if he was able to see how the other young couple interacted with each other, then maybe he could adjust a little to make their own interaction more normal... more loving.

The buggy ride was silent as usual, but Katie didn't mind because her heart was filled with hope. The farm *haus* was not as large as the one she lived in, but it was cozy and the couple was newly married so it was perfect. The farm was about half the size of the one Levi had but it was overrun by weeds and she could tell that he would have to spend a lot of hours there to get it done. But dropping by twice a week would get it done in *nee* time.

"I hear Jeremiah around back," Levi said as he tied off the horses. "Give Abigail my warm wishes."

"Okay."

She watched the back of his head disappear around the *haus* and shook her head. He was always focused on work. But at least now he was helping her *bruder*-in-law. The door flew open before she could knock and Abigail pulled her into a warm embrace.

"Katie!" she said. "It is so good to see you."

"You too. Let me look at you!"

They pulled away from each other and Katie examined her from head to toe, a huge smile on her face while she did so.

"You are glowing!" she said.

Abigail blushed.

"Come on inside and help me get the doughs in the oven," she said with a chuckle. But her brown eyes beamed with happiness.

"How many are you making?" Katie teased. "You already have a whole basket."

When she looked at Abigail she was nervously kneading bread, her eyes shifting from the bread to the wall.

"What is it?" Katie asked.

A deep sigh escaped her lips as she set the dough to rise and cleaned her hands.

"I do not know what else to do with myself. There is not much I can do on the farm now and everything is so new," she said.

"Why didn't you tell me before?"

"I didn't want to burden you."

"Abigail, you are my sister. You will never be a burden." This time it was Katie who initiated the hug, pulling her sister close and rubbing her back gently. "I am here for anything you need. Do you hear me?"

"*Jah.*"

When they broke apart, Katie quizzed Abigail on all the possible activities she could do around the *haus*. In what appeared to be a short time the bread was all done and it was time to make supper.

"Oh, I brought some things we can use for dinner. Things Levi likes."

"Let me see."

Abigail walked over to examine the contents of the basket while Katie emptied it onto the counter. There were jams and smoked meat cuts as well as some of the fruits they had growing on the farm.

"This is great. How about we get dinner ready together? The men will be hungry soon."

"You read my mind."

Dinner was on the table in under an hour and both women looked at their handiwork with pride. Katie felt her lips curve into a grin and her heart leaped with anticipation.

"Is this all an attempt to pull Levi closer to you?" Abigail asked suddenly.

Katie's breath hitched and her lips formed a line before she turned toward her sister.

"It is not," she stated, embarrassed, but hiding it well. "I just want the four of us to be friends. Is that such a bad thing?"

"*Nee,* it is not," Abigail responded hesitantly. She watched her sister closely for a few seconds, only giving up when the sound of the men's chatter drifted through the kitchen window.

"Wow, this looks amazing!" Jeremiah exclaimed when he pushed through the door, followed by Levi, who only nodded his agreement.

Everyone got seated at the table and the serving bowls were passed around so that each person could fill their plates with their favorites. Being in a group surely made dinner with Levi different because there was an actual conversation. Jeremiah spoke about the work they had gotten done on the farm and the future plans he had and even Levi chimed in a few times about the most efficient way to ensure productivity.

After the first night, they ended up going to the *haus* together biweekly so that Katie could catch up with Abigail while Levi worked. He seemed to be opening up to conversation during dinner but he would still remain silent at home and that only made her more confused about everything.

They were on their way home after visiting the Stoltz farm *haus*. Levi was focused on the road and Katie was itching to have a conversation, just the two of them.

"The board games were fun, weren't they?" she asked.

"*Jah.*"

She inhaled deeply and focused on the road too. Maybe everything was futile. He would never change and they would never get closer. Even though that was what her mind said, her heart was still hopeful.

"Jeremiah and Abigail seem to be really happy

together. You can see it in their smiles and the way they interact. Maybe one day we can know the same type of joy."

The horse snorted, but there was *nee* response from Levi. He only stared at the road in silence. Feeling disappointed Katie focused on her hands wishing they were home.

"Katie."

Her mouth popped open and she looked at Levi. Their eye met and her heart fluttered with hope again.

"I am fond of you..."

Her heart leaped as if it was attempting to burst from her chest and she reached for his hand, but he pulled away and shook his head.

Her eyes glossed over with tears and she looked away, hoping he did not see. Her stomach hurt from the rejection. She wanted to hide her sorrow, but she couldn't. Not yet.

"I was in love once before," Levi continued. "When I was living in Ohio. Her name was Rebecca and I was sure that we would get married. I was about to ask her to marry me when she took ill with a fever... she never recovered."

Her heart ached now. She couldn't imagine the pain Levi was feeling but her own heart understood a little better. He was hurting from a loss and that was why he could not open his heart.

"I understand, even though I have never lost someone I cared about so much. But remember that with *Gott* you can open your heart again. You can—"

"*Nee.*"

"I—"

"I have *nee* plans to risk my heart again, Katie. There is *nee* certainty in this life, so it is best to leave things as they are."

Before she could say anything else he got down from the buggy and unhitched the horses, walking them to the barn while she sat there staring after him. She got down from the buggy and walked inside, feeling as if she would lose her footing if she didn't get to her room quickly enough. As soon as she dropped into her chair, she heard the door to Levi's bedroom closed.

Her heart was broken. Although she had *nee* experience with a broken heart she recognized it. Tears trickled from her eyes, even as she closed them to stop them from flooding her face.

"*Gott*, please tell me what to do. I feel too broken to decide what to do next and then act on it. Why is this happening to me? Why does it always seem impossible for us to find love in this marriage?"

She changed into her nightgown and continued to pray. The hope she had was draining from her and she knew that once that was lost, so would her drive to try to change things.

But at this point, with everything Levi had said. It would take a miracle of unparalleled proportions for their marriage to transform into something loving.

CHAPTER FIVE

*S*ummer passed as quickly as it had come and when winter started, Katie felt as if it was reflecting the state of her marriage. The only light was the fact that Abigail had fallen pregnant and she could focus on the niece or nephew she was sure to welcome soon.

As the weather got harsher, Levi continued to help Jeremiah and Katie continued to accompany him so that she could see Abigail. The last time she was there she had to do all the cooking so that her sister could rest. Her belly was huge and there was *nee* way she could stand on her feet for too long. That made her grumpy, but Susannah assured them that it was perfectly normal for an expectant *mamm* to become irritable.

Katie was happy for her sister. She was married to a *mann* who loved her and a *boppli* was just a product of that love. Her hand stretched over her own belly as she thought about having *kinner*. She would never become a *mamm* unless she and Levi found a way to bring love into their marriage and they were far from it. She released a long sigh and reclined in the chair further as she pulled the book she was reading closer to her eyes. Maybe she could get lost in the pages.

But the book was about love and a happy marriage and so it only reminded her how much hers was failing when it compared to the others she had seen around her. Her parents were happy. Her sister and her husband were happy. The friends she went to school with were happy in their marriages and some even had two *kinner* already. She sighed loudly and almost dropped the book away in defeat when there was a sound at the door.

Knock knock!

Her eyes drifted to the door and she quietly put

down the book so that she could get up and see who was calling on them so late. Levi was not expecting anyone because he would have said so. And she wasn't expecting anyone either. Who would drop by someone's *haus* so late anyway?

Knock! Knock! Knock!

The knock was more frantic now and Levi came out of his room and headed for the door, his long legs getting him there before her. It was dark out and there was *nee* light on the outside. She stopped behind Levi so that he could take charge of the situation. When he swung the door open, Jeremiah was standing on the porch. His usually pleasant face was filled with dread and his hands were shaking.

"Abigail is going into labor now," he said.

"What?" Katie asked, pushing past Levi. "She is not due for another month."

"Well she is in labor and she told me to come to get you."

"Okay."

"Be quick, I had to leave her alone."

"What about the midwife?" Katie asked. She could not imagine how her sister must have felt to be alone. She had been in the room when one of her *ants* gave birth and she knew it was not a pleasant experience. A woman in labor needed a lot of support and she would make sure Abigail had that when she got there.

"I stopped at her *haus* first, she is out with another lady but she will be here as soon as she can."

"Great. I will put on something warmer."

The cold air from the outside rushed into the *haus* and she heard Jeremiah's teeth clatter.

"How about I drive?" Levi offered. "Jeremiah is way too nervous and I would like to see you both safely there."

"*Denke,*" Jeremiah said.

Katie only nodded and rushed to her room to get some warm clothes. When she returned to the living room both men were ready and Levi walked her to the buggy and helped her inside. With Levi pushing the horses, they got to the *haus* in a short time, but there was a buggy already there. Jeremiah jumped out of the buggy as soon as it came to a stop and Levi helped Katie down before securing the horses.

"Katie!" Sarah Beiler greeted her when she entered the *haus*. Jeremiah was already by Abigail's side trying to soothe her.

"Hello, Sarah. What are you doing here so late?"

"I was passing by when I had a feeling that I needed to call in. Abigail was alone and I found that she had gone into labor so I stayed."

"How is she doing?"

"She is almost ready to push, but having you and Jeremiah here is great for relaxing her."

"I am glad you are here," Katie told the other woman. Sarah smiled softly at her, understanding the anxiety behind her words.

"I do not have a lot of experience, but I can show you what I know until the midwife gets here."

"That sounds great."

"So how about I teach you so that you can deliver the

others when they come?" Sarah asked, smiling softly at Katie.

"There will be *nee* others if it will feel like this," Abigail protested.

Sarah smiled and Katie grinned at her sister through the bedroom door.

"Didn't you say you wanted to have five *kinner*?" she asked seriously, rubbing her chin to add effect.

"I have changed my mind!"

"But it is too late for that," Jeremiah teased.

But the look Abigail gave him stopped him in his tracks and he immediately left the teasing to the sisters.

Suddenly, Abigail's scream pierced through the silence of the night, and Katie rolled up her sleeves and followed Sarah's lead. They comforted Abigail as much as they could until the midwife arrived. The labor was long. Abigail was in pain but there was not much that they could do but wait. Jeremiah comforted her in every way he could and Katie tried to distract her from the pain. Even Levi helped, fetching water and fresh linens whenever there was a need.

"How much longer will this take?" Abigail asked through gritted teeth.

"*Not* very long," Jeremiah said.

But the midwife shook her head, it would be a while.

Everyone took turns sitting with Abigail throughout the night. Soon Susannah and James heard the news and they showed up too and tried to make her comfortable but nothing worked.

"Are first-time pregnancies always this difficult?" Katie asked the midwife when they had both stepped into the living room for a break.

"*Nee,*" the woman responded. "But I have seen longer labor. She will deliver the *boppli* soon."

An hour later, Abigail's screams echoed through the *haus*, and then it was replaced by the cry of a newborn *boppli*.

"It is a boy," the midwife announced.

Jeremiah's grin was so huge that it covered almost all his face and everyone in the *haus* erupted in cheers.

Katie helped the midwife to clean up the *boppli* while Jeremiah soothed his *fraa*. When the *boppli* was clean and wrapped in a new blanket she walked over to Abigail and handed him to her.

"Here is your *boppli*, my dear sister."

But when she tried to place the *boppli* in her arms, Abigail shook her head.

"*Nee*. I just want to rest," she said. "Let me rest first."

Katie glanced at the midwife and then Jeremiah. His face reflected the same confusion she was feeling. Abigail had been waiting for months to meet her *boppli*. Why didn't she want to hold him?

"She is exhausted after the long labor," the midwife suggested but there was something in her eyes she had seen this before. I am more than exhausted too, but I will fetch some milk and then I will come by to check on her tomorrow," she added before she left.

"Abigail, our son is here. Why don't you hold him a little and then you can sleep?"

"*Nee*. I just want to sleep," Abigail protested, her voice was weak but firm.

Katie watched the scene in silence, rocking the sleeping *boppli* in her arms. Sarah walked over to her and touched her on her arm while she peered down at the *boppli*.

"Why don't you go and introduce him to Levi, get him out of the room for a while?"

When she looked over at Abigail she knew that there was *nee* way she would change her mind so she agreed and Sarah held the door open so that she could leave.

"Everything will be okay, little one," she whispered to the *boppli*. "Your *mamm* will hold you soon. As soon as she gets some rest."

She rocked him gently and walked to the other end of the room where Levi was sitting. When he saw her, he stood up and placed a warm hand on her arm as he peered at the *boppli*.

"He is so precious," he said.

"*Jah*, he is. He is perfect," she said.

In that second she wondered what their *boppli* would look like and then stopped herself from thinking about it too much. It was too painful to focus on something that would likely never happen. It was a lot better to focus on what was happening at the moment as she held her beautiful nephew in her arms.

CHAPTER SIX

"**W**hat can I do?" Katie asked Jeremiah, Susannah, and Sarah as they all sat in the living room. Levi was hovering, obviously uncomfortable but wanting to support the *familye*. James was outside sitting on the porch. It all seemed to be too much for him so he preferred to stay alone.

"There is nothing we can do but wait," Sarah said.

"I have tried everything I could think of," Jeremiah explained, covering his face in his hands and rocking back and forth before he got up and started pacing the room.

"She wants nothing to do with the *boppli*," Susannah

said. Her voice cracked as she held back the tears that threatened to fall from her eyes. Katie reached across the couch to grasp her *mamm*'s hand and gently squeezed it.

"I don't think the *boppli* should stay in this *haus* while Abigail is like this," Sarah said. "Maybe if he stays somewhere else she will recover sooner."

"*Jah*, that is a good idea," Susannah agreed.

"Why is that good?" Jeremiah asked. "Should the *boppli* be here so we can ask her every day?"

"*Nee,*" Sarah answered. "I have seen this before, and trust me it will be better if the *boppli* is away, at least for a little while. We can get her checked out by the doctor to confirm but sometimes new *mamm*s experience depression and that can cause them to refuse to see or care for their *boppli*."

"This is normal?" Jeremiah asked, his eyes wide.

"For some *mamm*s."

"So how is it fixed?"

"We have to give her time. So, we can't try to force

45

her to take care of him. She will ask for him when she is ready."

"Okay," Jeremiah said, but confusion was written all over his face. He could not understand what was happening because he was too focused on taking care of his *familye*.

"Who will take care of him?" he asked.

"*Mamm*?"

Susannah shook her head and gripped Katie's hand.

"I do not remember how to care for a *boppli* so young and I will be too worried about Abigail to focus on him. It would be better if you take him."

"But I—"

"I am sure you will be great, Katie. And he will be great practice for when you have your own *boppli*."

She wanted to blurt out that she would never have a *boppli*, but it was not the right time and she could not tell every one of her shame. It was already embarrassing and she and Levi were the only ones who knew what their marriage was really like.

"I will get his things ready," Jeremiah said.

Her eyes met Levi's and he nodded. He didn't have to say anything for her to understand that he wanted whatever was best for the *boppli* and her sister. With his agreement, she went to help Jeremiah pack the *boppli*'s things and Levi took them to the buggy.

"Have you named him yet?" she asked Jeremiah as he passed the *boppli* to her. He had just woken up and as she held him, Levi took his cot to the buggy.

"We wanted to name our first-born son Adam," Jeremiah said. "Abigail is not responding about names right now, but it was what we decided, so that is his name."

"That is a beautiful name," Katie said. "I am sure she will get back to normal soon. I will not stop praying for her recovery.

"*Denke*, Katie. Please just take care of our son while I take care of my *fraa*."

"I will."

Jeremiah disappeared into the bedroom and they heard muffled sounds, but it was clear that he was trying to get Abigail to see the *boppli* again and she was refusing.

"I am your *ant*," Katie whispered to the *boppli*. "And I will take great care of you."

"Allow me to say goodbye," Susannah said as she got up and took Adam from Katie's arms. James came inside then.

"What is happening?" he asked.

"Adam is going home with Katie for a while," Susannah responded.

"We are hoping that with the *boppli* out of the *haus* Abigail's recovery will be easier and quicker."

He looked from one woman to the other but didn't say anything. When his eyes landed on the bedroom door, he went to the kitchen to get a coffee. James Raber was not a *mann* of many words, but Katie had never seen him so quiet. He was hurting for his daughter in a way she could not imagine and it pained him that he could not help her.

The drive home felt longer than usual because Adam was fussy and she could not get him to stop crying. Was taking him home a bad idea? She looked across at Levi and he was focused on the road as usual. So, she tried to focus on Adam, to figure out how to soothe him. But nothing seemed to work and she was near giving up when they got home. Levi helped her down from the buggy so that they could go and get warm inside while he brought in everything.

"Still *nee* luck?" Levi asked. He had just brought in the cot and placed it before the couch so that it was right before her. "Where should I put it?"

"In my room would probably be best, beside the bed."

"Okay."

Adam was still screaming at the top of his lungs. *Nee* matter what she did he didn't stop and she was getting weary. She was pacing when Levi walked over to her and reached out his hands.

"How about you give me a try?" he asked.

A lazy smile stretched across her lips as she handed the *boppli* to him and all but dropped into the couch, her eyes closing as she tried to fight the exhaustion. But then everything went silent.

Katie's eyes fluttered open and she looked around the room for Levi and Adam but they were nowhere to be seen. But then she heard Levi's voice coming from his room when she got closer to the door she saw him sitting in a chair with Adam nestled in his arms. He was telling the *boppli* a story and it seemed to captivate him. He was so gentle. Katie had never seen him that way before and the entire scene caused her heart to swell with admiration. She smiled at him and leaned against the doorframe. Her hand slipped to her own belly and she sighed softly. He had a father's touch, but at this rate, he was not going to be a father, and neither would she be a *mamm*.

"The little Amish boy wanted a toy more than anything, he said. "But he didn't know how to make one so he went all around the community to find someone who could help him."

Katie smiled at them as she got more comfortable to watch. She had never seen Levi like this and there was *nee* way she would take her eyes off him for even a second.

"When he finally found someone who could teach him how to make toys he carved a toy horse. And he was so proud of it. He had done it himself after learning how to carve and he wanted to keep it forever. But one day he was with his *mamm* in the town and he saw another boy who was playing with a box. He asked him why he was playing with the box and the little boy said it was because he didn't have any toys. The little Amish boy was so touched that he gave the horse to the other boy. His *mamm* was so happy about his choice that she told everyone about it. A week later all the carpenters in town started to drop by his *haus* with toys they made for him. His one act of kindness was returned tenfold and now he had a lot more toys to give away."

The story made Katie smile and she wondered if the little boy was Levi. She never thought him capable of such gentleness but here he was proving her wrong and tugging at her heartstrings in ways she never thought possible.

Silence filled the *haus* as Adam finally drifted off to sleep and Levi looked up to meet her eyes. She thought she saw him blush, but it all happened so quickly that she was not certain she had really seen it. She beckoned to him and he stood with Adam and followed her to her room where he deposited the *boppli* in the cot and watched him for a little while with satisfaction on his face.

They closed the door behind them when they left

and hoped that he would sleep long enough to not be so cranky when he awoke.

"Do you want some tea?" she asked.

"Jah. Denke."

Katie went to the kitchen to warm the water and start gathering the ingredients.

"You have been very supportive through all of this, Levi. I appreciate it a lot because I do not know what I would have done if you were not here. This is all so hard to understand. *Denke.*"

"You are welcome, Katie. I hope that Abigail recovers before Christmas so that she can truly enjoy the treasure that is her firstborn," he said.

"I hope so too," Katie agreed. "I hope that *Gott* helps her to pull through so that she can see what a blessing little Adam is."

Her heart beat faster and she felt a drive deep inside her that she could not explain. She walked to the carpet in the living room and kneeled, looking up at the ceiling before closing her eyes and focusing on *Gott.*

"Please *Gott*," she said. "Help Abigail to rediscover her strength. Help her to fight through this depression and focus on the people who love her. Help her to overcome this. Give Abigail her own Christmas miracle."

She felt Levi's hand cover hers before she heard his voice echoing her words.

"...her own Christmas miracle."

Katie opened her eyes and their eyes locked. His eyes were as pained as she knew hers were. He wanted her sister to recover as badly as she did and that made her appreciate him more. She closed her eyes again and focused on praying for her sister's recovery.

"She is a strong woman, she always has been and I know that she gets her strength from You, *Gott*. Please help her to recover so that she can care for her son as a *mamm* should. Little Adam deserves to have his *mamm* in his life so that he can grow up with all the Amish values *mamm*s are charged with teaching. We will take care of him as much as we need to but he needs his *mamm's* love and I need my sister. I need her to be okay."

She also prayed that she and Levi would be able to properly care for Adam so that he would be a healthy *boppli* when he returned home. Levi's fingers wrapped around hers and she felt his strength flow into her as she continued to pray. He was taking a step that she had only ever dreamed and prayed for and she appreciated it and wanted to savor it for all that it was but her focus had to remain on her sister's recovery and Adam.

CHAPTER SEVEN

"*I* do not want to see him," Abigail said.

Katie held the *boppli* in her arms and listened, hoping that Abigail would change her mind but remaining very doubtful that would happen.

"I failed the *boppli* by bringing him into the world too soon," Abigail continued, her voice was loud but she wasn't angry. Katie could hear the pain in her voice and it broke her heart. Her sister was the most loving person she had ever known and she was always the person she could rely on for a positive response to anything and yet now she seemed as if she had lost all her joy for life. It was as if she didn't have the strength to do anything, even get out of bed.

Jeremiah came out of the room and closed the door behind him gently. It had been about a week and there was *nee* progress that anyone could see. *Nee* one could convince Abigail otherwise. She would talk to Katie about anything except Adam and Jeremiah still could not soothe her soul. *Nee* words could do that, so they all continued to pray for her recovery.

"*Denke* for looking after Adam," he said. "I have *nee* idea when she will recover her senses, but I pray that it will be soon. I want my *familye* back together."

"It will happen," Levi said, resting his hand on the other man's shoulder. "Nothing is lost yet."

"I really hope you are right, Levi. It hurts me to see her like this, knowing what she had wanted and that I can't help her."

"Just be grateful that you still have her. Do not lose hope and in time everything will be okay."

Katie listened to the men and hope formed in her heart, not only for Abigail's recovery but for her marriage to improve. She had *nee* idea Levi was so hopeful and it gave her new respect for him, renewing her own hope that he would see her differently in time. All she had to do was be patient.

They went home soon after though they didn't like leaving Jeremiah alone with Abigail in that state. For the next few days, they traded taking care of Adam. They managed to keep Adam content, learning his needs, and taking care of them with ease. Katie had formed a bond with the boy and it brought light to her life every day. Soon she noticed that Levi had formed the same bond with Adam and it was starting to extend to her.

"He prefers you," she said. "Maybe you need to teach me one of your songs."

"So, you can take away his favor?" Levi teased.

"We can share it," she said, casually shrugging as if she wasn't being serious.

Levi looked at her and tilted his head from side to side.

"If I teach you a song will you do two more nappy changes per day?"

"I will."

"Okay. I will write it for you and we can sing it together until you learn it."

Adam awoke when Levi was in the middle of writing the lyrics for the song that often put him to bed. Katie went to get the *boppli* from the cot and rocked him gently while she got his milk and tried to feed him. But he refused to take the bottle.

"I think he wants you," she said.

"Great. I just finished writing the song. So, let us trade."

Adam fit snuggly in Levi's arms and Katie started scanning the paper. She did not have the best singing voice and Levi had not heard it before so she was feeling kind of nervous. She watched as Adam's lips curled around the bottle and he started to drink his milk. She shrugged and shook her head and Levi chuckled.

"You do not have to be the best at everything," he teased.

"But I am supposed to have maternal instincts," she said.

"And I am supposed to have paternal instincts, right?" he asked.

She shook her head and laughed. "I have never heard of that."

"Well here is the proof."

They were a happy little *familye*, or so they would appear to someone who didn't know that Adam was her nephew. Levi was a lot happier and a lot more talkative and his joy was starting to become contagious. She was worrying less about Abigail though she prayed for her every day. She was more hopeful now that she would recover. She had to.

She watched as Levi sang Adam to bed and her heart beat fast with admiration for him. She found herself imagining what it would be like to have her own *boppli*, how involved Levi would be, and how caring he would be as a *daed*. She smiled at the thought and he raised his eyebrows at her as he walked over to where she was standing.

"What is so funny?" he asked.

She feigned ignorance and shrugged.

"I don't know," she said and Levi chuckled softly.

"*Denke* for helping out with everything." The seriousness of her words carried in her voice and Levi became serious too, looking at her curiously.

"You are welcome. I never thought that I was capable of so much charity. I never thought I had it within me."

"Well, I am glad that you do."

"Me too. But I think Adam is responsible for awakening it. It must have been lying dormant in my soul for a long time because I can't remember a time when I was this willing to help others when I enjoyed it so much. But somehow the *boppli* found his way to my heart."

"I am glad that someone made their way there," she said. "Though I believe it would have happened eventually, with or without Adam."

"You see a lot in me, don't you?"

Katie gulped and just stood there staring at Levi. What was she supposed to say? If she said *jah*, he would probably give her a lecture on expecting too much and tell her that their relationship would never change. And if she told him no, he would probably shrug it off and they would never speak about it again. Did he really want an answer?

The way he stared at her, his eyes searching as if trying to get into her soul, caused her to gasp softly. She forced a smile to her lips, unable to break away from his gaze, and took a step back.

"Goodnight, Levi," she said as she made to close the door.

But he caught her hand suddenly and she felt a current like fire flow through her. He stepped closer to her to close the space and bent down so that he could whisper in her ear, his warm breath tickling her skin caused her to shiver with hope.

"I would prefer that we not spend the night in separate rooms."

Her breath hitched as she looked at him and she was unable to speak for a few seconds.

"What..." she gulped. She was imagining it all, right? But if it was all in her mind, why was he staring at her like that, with so much desire?

"What do you have in mind?" she asked, clearing her throat.

She was nervous. Her hand shivered but she was not cold and her heart beat hard against her chest. Levi was so close to her. And he was touching her. The way he was looking at her suggested that he wanted her. That he wanted his *fraa*. And she was too surprised to react in the way she had always dreamed. But she was happy.

When his arm wound around her she leaned into him and allowed him to lead her to his bedroom. When he closed the door, her cheeks turned pink and she smiled at her husband shyly.

"Come to me," he said and she walked over to him. he took off her cap and undid her hairpin so that her brown hair flowed over her shoulders and he stared at her as if he was seeing her for the first time.

"You are beautiful," he said before he leaned in and kissed her lips, softly. Then she wound her hands around his neck and the kiss deepened. For the first time since they got married the year before, they went to bed together.

A cry pierced through the darkness and Katie's eyes fluttered open. It took her a few seconds to remember that she was in Levi's bed and that made her smile. She left the room silently hoping not to wake him up and stopped in her tracks when she saw Levi with the *boppli* in his arms, already giving him a bottle. He smiled when he saw her and she returned a huge grin. Not wanting to disturb their rhythm she sat on the couch and watched him.

When he grew tired of standing he sat down on the couch beside her and she rubbed Adam's tiny arm until he drifted off to sleep. She took the bottle and Levi laid the sleeping *boppli* on his shoulder and rubbed his back softly until a soft burp left his little mouth. Gently taking Adam, she placed him in his cot again and returned to find Levi still on the couch so she sat beside him again. Outside it was *nee* longer dark and she could see the red of the sunrise in the distance.

"I never thought that I could feel this way again," he said.

Her breath hitched as she looked at him, with her

eyes wide open. He chuckled when he saw her expression and pulled her closer to him.

"I never thought that I could love again."

She gulped and just sat in silence, not wanting to break the spell of the moment.

"If I am being honest, I have been feeling safe with you for quite some time, but I was afraid to give in to it. Now I only want the feeling to continue. If you want the same thing."

Katie's mouth opened but there was *nee* sound, so she nodded and Levi smiled at her. He pulled her closer and she curled into his side.

"I have felt comfortable with you for a long time too," she finally said. "And I am happy that we got here so that we can know how each other feels."

"Me too." He leaned down to kiss her but there was suddenly a knock at the door.

"Are you expecting anyone?" he asked.

"*Nee.*"

"Okay. Stay here and I will see who it is."

The door pulled open to reveal a beaming Susannah and James. She hugged Levi and rushed in to hug Katie as they both looked at her in silence.

"What is it, *mamm*?" she asked. "What is going on? Is Abigail okay?"

"She is better than okay," she said. "She is finally ready to hold her son."

Katie shrieked and hugged her *mamm* again, happiness flowing through her. But then her eyes locked with Levi's and something shifted. Their little makeshift *familye* was being broken up. What did that mean for them? Was the connection that had started to create able to survive such a huge change.

The look on his face seemed to mirror all the fears coursing through her and Katie hoped that what they had found with each other was enough. It had to be enough.

Please, Gott.

CHAPTER EIGHT

*S*ince Adam was asleep, Katie and Levi agreed to bring him to his *mamm's* as soon as he woke up. Susannah and James left them so that they could be with their recovered daughter and Katie was left alone with Levi to tend to her developing sadness. She was happy that Abigail had recovered. It was all she had been praying for. And since that morning was Christmas Eve, she had recovered just in time to have her first Christmas with Adam.

She walked over to the couch and sat down, gazing at the wall and not seeing anything. She knew that Levi had opened up because of Adam. Caring for the *boppli* had caused him to set free the side of him that he had always kept hidden and now that Adam was to be returned to his parents she feared that Levi would close up again.

The connection she had finally formed was slipping away and there wasn't anything she could do about it. She had *nee* idea how long she was sitting there.

"*Gott* answered our prayers," Levi said as he sat down beside her.

He seemed to be flipping through the book he had been reading for the last week without seeing the pages and she wondered if he was as distracted as she was. But there was *nee* way to be sure and she couldn't believe that he was. He had never wanted them to fall in love and have a normal married life. He had never asked her to be more than they were. Levi was always okay with them being civil to each other as he mourned the death of his first love.

Was the connection between them even real? It never happened until they had to take care of Adam together. So now that Adam was going back to his parents, would the connection fade?

Too distracted by her thoughts, Katie got up and walked to the kitchen, searching for something to focus on instead of the thoughts swirling through her mind. She found some flour and then grabbed a few other ingredients. She would bake a cake. Baking always cleared her mind. She could focus on getting the perfect taste and the perfect texture.

In only a few minutes she had the batter ready and she placed it in the wood-burning oven to bake. As soon as she *nee* longer had a distraction her mind went back to analyzing the state of their relationship. There was *nee* way to avoid it when all she had wanted was for them to get close and now that they had that it was being threatened.

She took the cake from the oven and placed it on a cooling rack and focused on making the frosting next. But that only took a few minutes. Soon her mind was clear again and there was nothing else for her to do.

When Adam stirred and started to cry she went to him and took care of him. By the time she returned from the room, Levi had the horse harnessed to the buggy and was already dressed for the trip. He didn't say anything. He had not said much since her parents dropped by and that only worried her more. He was obviously ready to return the *boppli* to Abigail and Jeremiah and there seemed to be nothing else to it.

"Can you hold him while I get dressed?" she asked Levi.

He nodded and took Adam from her arms, cradling him gently and walking him around the room. She heard the first few notes of his favorite lullaby before she closed the door and focused on getting dressed. It was the only thing in her control at that moment.

The drive to the Stoltz's *haus* felt like an hour but it was only a few minutes. The wind was cold and it was blowing hard as if there was a storm on the horizon, but they made it safely. Levi was always a careful driver so she was not worried about making it to their destination. They were silent and that brought back memories of how everything was before Adam came into their lives. Levi focused intently on the road and she could not coax him into a conversation *nee* matter how hard she tried so she gave up and focused on Adam alone.

When they pulled up to the *haus*, Levi got down and tied the horses and then helped Katie down. Before her feet touched the ground, Abigail rushed out of the *haus* and hugged her gently before slipping her hands around Adam's tiny body and taking him not her arms.

"*Denke*, Katie," she said, her eyes filled with tears that started to flow freely down her cheeks. Her lips trembled as she tried to find more words of gratitude and so Katie rested her hand on her shoulder and squeezed.

"You would have done the same for me."

Abigail nodded and Katie wrapped her arm around her and led her back to the warmth of the living room. When she stepped into the room she saw that her parents were there, as well as Amos and Sarah Beiler.

"Did Christmas Eve... the celebrations start early?" she asked teasingly.

"There is a lot to celebrate," Jeremiah said, beaming with pride and joy as he watched his *fraa* and *boppli*.

Katie felt a sharp pain in her stomach as she watched

the scene before her. She was happy. She was sure that she was happy for Abigail. But didn't she deserve to be happy too? She was trying to rein in her thoughts when Sarah and Amos approached her and Levi who had slipped inside and stood beside her.

"You both did an amazing job stepping in and caring for little Adam," Amos said.

"He was well looked after. I can tell those things just by the way a *boppli*'s eyes glisten," Sarah added, playfully.

Levi glanced at Katie before he looked at the couple as if he expected her to answer for them. But she didn't. Instead, she took off in tears, leaving him confused. She walked as far as her feet could carry her, which was only a few steps from the porch, and she just stood there looking at nothing in particular, the tears rolling down her cheeks. She heard the footsteps behind her and felt her body go tense. She was not in the mood to talk to anyone, especially Levi. But when the person got closer she realized that it was Sarah.

"What is going on?" Sarah asked, her eyebrows

bunched up as she looked at Katie and tried to get Katie to open up.

Releasing a sigh that seemed to struggle to escape from her lips, Katie looked at Sarah with an expression she knew would reflect the brokenness she felt inside and confessed.

"I am guilty of the sin of envy," she said.

Sarah came closer to her and rested her hand on her shoulder.

"Why do you say that?"

"Because I want my marriage to continue to flourish," she said.

"I don't understand."

"I want what Abigail and Jeremiah have. Even when she was sick he was by her side because he loves her. Levi and I do not have that. We never did... until Adam came home with us and he started to open up."

"Oh, I see."

"But now that Adam is gone everything will go back

to how it was and there was *nee* love in that. I don't want a civil marriage. I never did."

Katie felt the sobs before she heard them and Sarah pulled her into a hug so that she could sob softly in her arms.

"You can build on the feelings you discovered when Adam was with you," Sarah said as she tried to soothe her. "The *boppli* wasn't the cause of the feelings, Katie," She said, patting her back gently. "Maybe he was the catalyst that brought it to the surface but the feelings came from you both."

"Everything will go back to the way it was," she cried. "He won't be able to remember and things will not continue."

"Just give it a chance," Sarah insisted gently. "Things will be different because Adam is not there anymore. But that doesn't mean that it has to go back to the way it was."

Katie stepped away from her embrace and wiped her eyes. She didn't believe that things could still continue the way they were going, but she wanted to trust that it would. That meant she had to rely on *Gott.* If Abigail recovered before Christmas, there was a chance she and Levi could make love the foundation of their marriage, right? The doubt still lingered in her mind.

"When you go home you can both talk about it and see what happens," Sarah suggested.

"*Jah*, maybe we should talk. But what if he doesn't want to talk?"

"I am sure he will."

"*Nee*. He will just disappear and then ignore me when I try to talk about it at home. Levi is not someone who likes to discuss his feelings."

"And are you?"

"Well..." No, she wasn't. And yet here she was sharing everything with Sarah when she had not even told her own *mamm*.

"Just talk to him."

"Okay. I will."

When her eyes were dry, Sarah wrapped her arms around Katie's shoulder and led her back to the *haus*. Katie felt the anxiety she had been holding inside fading in the cool air, but when they got closer to the *haus.* She realized that the buggy was gone and Levi was nowhere in sight. All the fears Katie had about his feeling reverting to the previous state of their marriage again and she realized that she had to talk to him. Whatever the outcome she needed him to know that her feelings for him had always been there.

CHAPTER NINE

Katie felt her anxiety take over as she looked around and confirmed that Levi was gone. He was not outside and when she went inside and looked around he could not be found anywhere. She wanted to run after him, although she had *nee* idea where he went. But she managed to regain control.

"We will take you home since it is on our way," Sarah said to her and Katie nodded. She was happy that she had people who were still looking out for her. Since Abigail had just recovered she had decided to give the couple some time alone to bond with their son and Levi had agreed.

Just thinking about him made her heart ache and her

eyes threatened to well up with tears again. All she *need*ed to do was bid everyone farewell, so she went over to her sister first and pulled her into a hug, careful not to squish Adam who was still nestled in her arms.

"I am happy you are okay now," she whispered. "I missed you."

She then kissed Adam on his forehead and watched as his *mamm* rocked him in her arms. He seemed to know that he was with his *mamm*. There was *nee* fussing and he cooed softly as if trying to convey his thanks to her.

"*Denke*, Katie," Abigail said when their eyes met.

"It was *nee* problem."

"But to ask Levi to step in..."

"He enjoyed it very much, so it was not a problem."

Abigail's face lit up and Katie nodded her confirmation.

"I am sorry I missed that," Abigail said, "Levi with a *boppli*."

"I will arrange it for you," Katie said with a chuckle

as she leaned in to hug her sister again. "I will be sure to visit you again soon. But I have to get home."

"I understand. I hope it all works out."

Katie raised her eyebrows in question and Abigail laughed. Shaking her head, she told her parents goodbye and headed outside towards the Beiler's waiting buggy. The drive was short, but she felt her teeth clatter for the entire journey and her hands kept fiddling with each other, a clear sign of her nervousness. Sarah kept giving her encouraging looks but they did not help. She had *nee* idea if Levi was at the *haus* and if he was, she had *nee* idea what she was going to say to him. But she knew some things had to be said. She had to try to save the bond they had created, to maintain the affection in their marriage. Love.

Wait? Did she love him? Her eyes widened as she thought about it. The way she missed him whenever he wasn't around, the way she thought about him even when she was supposed to be focused on something else that needed her attention.

In just a few minutes she was in front of her *haus*. The buggy was parked so Levi was home. But the anxiety she felt stopped her from getting down from the buggy and running into the *haus*.

The warm hand on her shoulder squeezed her gently and Katie turned around to look at Sarah whose head was leaning to the side as she observed her.

"Keep the faith and go on in," she said. "Whatever *Gott* wants to be will be. Just have faith that it will be *gut*."

"I will try."

While the buggy moved away from the *haus*, Katie walked slowly toward the front door. She took a deep breath when her hands touched the handle and then pushed the door open. Levi was standing in the middle of the living room, facing her. He was wearing a fine suit and he held two candles in his hands, one lit and one not.

Her brows furrowed as she wondered what was happening, unable to move from the spot she was standing in. But she was able to close the door behind her to block out the cold breeze that was beating against her back and causing her legs to shake.

"Hello, Katie." His voice was different. It sounded raw with emotion and it even cracked a little although he only said two words.

"Hi," she responded, still confused. What was he doing? Why did he have candles?

"I spoke to Amos when you were talking to Sarah outside," he said.

She looked him in the eyes and he stared at her the same way he had looked at her the night before. Her mouth dropped open as his lips curved into a smile and she took a step toward him.

"Why?"

"I was also sad at the thought of things changing between us," he said. He moved from side to side on the ball of his feet and averted his gaze a little but then he met her eyes again and she saw more emotion than she had ever seen him express. "I thought that I would lose you. Everything we have now came about because Adam was here and now he is gone. Without Adam's presence, I feared that you would change your mind about me."

She gulped but she did not say anything. Was she

dreaming or was this all happening? How could he be saying the same things that were on her mind? The same things that had caused her great anxiety earlier.

"I want to nurture the new bond we have and see how it might blossom, Katie. I want to have a real marriage."

The heartbeat in her chest was so fast she could hardly hear the words that left his lips. But she heard enough to know that he wanted them to cherish what had developed between them.

"Are you sure?" she asked. "You told me before that you could never love again."

He took a step toward her. He was close enough to touch her but his hands were away from her, the hand with the lit candle lighting up between them.

"I am sure. I have fallen in love with you."

"How do you know."

"I just know. I have never felt this way about anyone before. I thought that what I had felt for Rebecca was love, but it wasn't. Because it didn't come close to what I feel whenever I think about you. The joy I feel when I remember that you are already my *fraa*."

"You won't change your mind?"

"*Nee.*" He chuckled and she squinted her eyes as she stared at him.

"What is so funny?" she asked softly.

"I thought I was the skeptic and here you are asking the same questions I would have asked a few months ago."

Katie smiled as she thought about it. He was right.

"I just want to make sure you love me."

"I love you. And I will always love you. And I want to create a marriage filled with love and *kinner* and happiness." Levi reached out his hand with the unlit candle. "Do you want the same thing?"

"*Jah.*"

"I wanted to do this to show you how much I care. My love for you is like a flame and that is represented by this candle... I want to know if you feel the same. If you do light your candle."

Everything she had ever wanted was happening and she could not find the right words to tell Levi how she felt about him. Levi placed the unlit candle in her hand and their hands touch for a few seconds, sending a current through her that made her gasp. At first, she couldn't move and she could see the hope dying in his eyes through the flickering flame. A smile came to her lips and she touched her candle to his, lighting the flame that represented her love. Their eyes met over the candlelight.

"I love you too," she finally said.

He smiled at her then, his eyes lighting up, and her lips curved into a smile too. Holding the candles carefully, they stepped closer to each other and held each other in a tender embrace.

CHAPTER TEN

"**C**an you believe it has been a year already?" Levi asked as he turned the buggy onto the road that would lead to the Stoltz's *haus*.

"I can't. But it has been a very *gut* year," Katie replied to her husband.

"It will be very special won't it?" he teased.

"Just as this year is special," she said.

"Because we are together, truly together?"

"*Jah*."

The front yard already had a few parked buggies by

the time they arrived. Levi tied the horses and helped his *fraa* down, walking with her to the porch. Before they could knock Abigail pulled the door opened and Katie fell into her arms.

"It is so great to see you!" she said.

"Didn't you see me last week?" Abigail asked, raising an eyebrow.

"You know today is special," Katie teased.

Adam wobbled over and Levi picked him up in his arms and hugged him before passing him on to Katie. She hugged her nephew, tickling him so that he filled the room with giggles. Adam had just learned how to walk, but he was not talking yet. He had thrived since returning to his parents and in only a year their bond was so great that *nee* one would have known the trouble they had started out with.

"How are you doing my favorite nephew," she asked.

Bababbadogoda

"I think that is 'I am doing great," Levi offered.

"Or was it 'I want to go on the floor?" Abigail asked as she reached for her son. She placed him on the floor and he scampered away. "He has been running around as much as he could ever since he figured out how to walk."

"I guess it is time for you to have another then?" Katie teased.

"*Nee,*" Abigail replied quickly. Her brown eyes were serious and Katie thought she saw some fear behind them but she wasn't sure.

"Katie," James said as he walked over to them. He hugged her before turning to Levi and after that Susannah appeared to do the same.

"You came just in time," Susannah said.

"Just in time for what?"

"The food," she teased.

Jeremiah's *familye* was there too and they came over when they saw that Katie and Levi had arrived. When they had greeted everyone, Levi found Katie a chair and she sat down and watched Adam play.

"It is time for dinner and the homemade gifts exchange," Jeremiah announced a few minutes later.

Levi helped her to stand up and led her to the huge

table that had been added to just so that the whole *familye* could do it together. When she was comfortable, he sat in the chair next to her and waited on everyone else to join them.

"A special thanks to our parents and *ant*s for preparing the meal," Abigail said after everyone was seated.

"You just love your *mamm*'s cooking" Susannah teased.

"Susannah is the best cook I know," James added.

Everyone chuckled and then when the jokes were done the *familye* prayed together for getting to live for the year and the many blessings they received collectively. After that everyone was allowed to eat, even Adam who guarded a turkey leg as if he had been eating meat all his life.

"Who wants to open their gift first?" Jeremiah asked when the desserts were served and people were catching up.

"I would like to give this gift to Adam," Levi announced.

Everyone watched as he handed a parcel to Abigail.

She unwrapped it and found a carved wooden horse that Adam immediately took from her hands, causing everyone at the table to laugh.

"He loves it," Abigail said through her own chuckles. "*Denke*, Levi."

"I never saw you working on that?" Katie said to him in a whisper.

"I wanted to surprise you too."

She raised her eyebrows at him. "The story you told Adam about the little boy who wanted to make his own toy. It was you?"

"*Jah*. And now I will make a toy every month if I have to so that our *kinner* never want for anything."

"Did Adam make any presents?" Peter Stoltz asked. He was Jeremiah's younger *bruder* who looked just like him with the same blond hair and blue eyes.

Everyone chuckled again and Jeremiah shook his head at his *bruder*, a smile on his lips.

. . .

"Adam is a gift," Katie said and everyone turned to look at her. "He came into the world early and not only did he survive, but he helped others too. He was not born on Christmas, but he gave Abigail the strength to recover for Christmas, and having him in our home brought Levi and me closer. Without him, I have *nee* idea where we would be right now so for us he is one of the greatest gifts we have ever gotten."

"A true Christmas Miracle," Levi added.

"My miracle," Abigail said, kissing her son on the forehead.

"How about you open my gift?" Susannah said as she passed a parcel to Abigail. When she opened it she gasped at the small quilt? It was covered in the *familye* names and a beautiful vine ran through it.

"Adam will love this when he can understand," she said.

"Can I see it?" Jeremiah's *mamm* asked and Abigail passed it down to her.

"Weren't we supposed to make one gift?" James asked.

"Plus, one for Adam," Susannah said and everyone laughed.

Adam received a gift from everyone, from homemade toys to books he would not be able to read yet since he wasn't even talking. But he was happy to play with them all. After dessert, everyone gathered to sing Christmas hymns and Levi and Katie slipped away to the porch. He helped her to sit down and then joined her, and they both looked out at the trees that rustled in the whistling wind.

He placed his hand on her tummy and she placed her hand over his, smiling at his touch.

"I am glad that I opened my heart again, Katie. And because of you, I have already opened it again for the *boppli* we will have soon, come next Christmas he or she will celebrate with us and our *familye* will be complete."

Warmth coursed through her as her husband told her how he felt. She never got tired of hearing it. "I am glad you opened your heart too," she said. "I have never been happier."

"And we will be even more content when our son is born."

Katie raised her eyebrows and stared at her smiling husband. "How are you so sure it will be a boy?"

"I just sense it."

"And if it is a girl?"

"Then I will love her as much as I love you... or maybe more," he teased.

Katie shook her head at Levi and pulled him in close for a kiss. She could never get used to kissing her husband or having him hold her. She had found the love she had always longed for in her marriage.

AMISH CHRISTMAS CELEBRATION PREVIEW

Amish Christmas Celebration Preview

The air felt crisp and cool, like the sheet of ice that formed over the puddles and pond after the first chill of winter. Hannah Burkholder opened the front door with her left hand and carried the tin bucket with her right. The milk in the bucket sloshed as she set it on the counter. She quickly rushed to the door and shut it, trying desperately to keep the leftover warmth in their small *haus*. It had cooled considerably during the night but it was much warmer than the crisp December breeze outside.

Hannah was filling the last bottle of milk when her husband, Joseph walked into the kitchen. She quickly reached over to a dish on the counter and pulled off the cloth towels that she had draped over it. Before going out to get milk for their morning *kaffe*, she had made breakfast – his favorite.

"Breakfast smells wonderful," he said. Early in the morning, his normally deep voice was a little gravelly and sounded crankier than normal. They were still a young couple, having only been married for a year. However, Joseph's deep voice and aloof personality reminded her of some of the older men in the community – and Faith's Creek, Pennsylvania had its fair share of disgruntled old men.

She smiled sweetly at him. "*Jah,* I've made a breakfast bake this morning," she said. "I know how much you love it."

He sat down at the small breakfast table and nodded. Joseph's eyes moved toward the window as he took a deep breath. "The nights are beginning to get colder. The morning air feels cooler as well. It might be a harsh winter."

Hannah cut a piece of the casserole and placed it on a plate for him. "It's going to snow. I can feel it in the air. We will have a snowy Christmas this year. I hope that it won't ruin our plans if it gets too bad. We've never had to cancel a Christmas service before."

He let out a chuckle. "You were like this last year. You're as giddy as a child whenever Christmas comes and even more so when it snows." He let out a deep breath. "Don't worry about the service. I'm sure that it will be fine. Bishop Amos will do a wonderful job and we'll both get to enjoy it." He took a sip from his cup.

She sighed. "I love Christmas. There is something about the warmth at the service closest to Christmas Day and the celebration during Second Christmas."

"We're adults now, Hannah. I realize that you enjoy time with *familye* and celebrations but don't you think that you should start looking at life a little more seriously?"

Hannah nodded. "I suppose." She could feel a pang in her heart though for he had mentioned this a few times since they wed two summers ago. She cut herself a slice of her breakfast bake and waited for Joseph to bow his head. Together they said grace before she began to eat.

She looked at her husband, his cheeks were rosy and

she knew he had already been out in the stalls. First, he would make sure that the livestock was safe and warm and then he would walk the pasture to make sure that there was nothing wrong with the property. She felt that it was the least that she could do, to wait for him before she took a bite – though she didn't think that he realized she did that just for him.

Throughout breakfast, there were few words said. It wasn't until he had finished that he asked her about her day. "I assume that you're going to help Bishop Amos with the preparations for the district's Christmas service today."

"Yes, it's only four days away and there is so much left to do. I think there is some mending to do as well and..."

"There is mending to do here as well. Don't forget about that." He sounded annoyed.

"Oh, of course not. I plan on darning a few things this afternoon after I get back."

"I'll be back for dinner," he said as he put on a coat and took a step toward the door. He paused before opening it. "H-Have a good day," he said. "I'll see you tonight."

"Yes, a good day to you too." She looked at the back of his head and remembered, "Oh, I made you lunch." Hannah took a bag from the counter and handed it to him. "I hope you like it."

He took the bag from her and looked her in the eye. His gaze was often intense and could be somewhat uncomfortable but it was strangely soft this morning. "*Denke*," he said. "I appreciate everything that you do." He kissed her forehead and walked out the door, with the bag in his big, rough hand.

Hannah nearly melted as she stood, dumbfounded, by the doorway. It felt strangely warm in the cool kitchen all of a sudden. The loving gesture was so unexpected, for a moment it made her feel young and innocent once again. She could feel her heart and mind open up a little each day that they were together.

At first, Anna had had her trepidations. When she was younger, she had seen Joseph around the community and both of their families knew each other well. However, she had only spoken with Joseph a handful of times before it was decided that they should wed. She was three years his junior and they had little in common.

He was often cold and emotionally detached. None the less, she tried her best to keep a clean and warm home for him. They talked every now and then but they were never the heartfelt conversations that her parents had. When she approached her *mamm* about it, she merely told Hannah that the love would come in time. They needed to be able to find their place in the community and build their own home first. After that comes love and all the joys that follow it. Anna hoped so for life without love was as cold as the winter frost.

Shaking herself from her dreaming, she quickly put away the rest of the breakfast and adjusted the *kapp* on her head before dusting off her blue dress and walking out the door. As she rushed onto the porch, she double-checked to make sure that her auburn hair was still tucked into place and that she had her favorite sewing pouch in her pocket.

She liked to be the first at the church gatherings so that she could spend a little extra time in prayer before helping with the various tasks that needed to get done. Being a married woman who didn't need any more schooling or to take care of any children, she had the extra time. Some of the other women in the group suggested that before she had any children, she should spend extra time perfecting her sewing and finding her way around the community. There seemed to be a theme though she wasn't really sure what the right answer was or what everyone was getting at.

The sun rose above the hills in the distance, painting the fields with a splash of orange before brightening her world with waves of color and warming the air. Little did she know that the clouds in the distance would end up changing her life so dramatically. The clouds would bring the change that she would need in order to see the path that had been laid out in front of her.

Read this amazing value set of 20 Amish romances for FREE with Kindle Unlimited. Grab Amish Christmas Celebration now

follow button

+ Follow

This book is dedicated to the wonderful Amish people and the faithful life that they live.

Go in peace my friends.

As an independent author, Sarah relies on your support. If you enjoyed this book, please leave a review on Amazon or Goodreads.

ABOUT THE AUTHOR

Sarah Miller was born in Pennsylvania and spent her childhood close to the Amish people. Weekends were spent doing chores; quilting or eventually babysitting in the community. She grew up to love their culture and the simple lifestyle and had many Amish friends. The one thing that you can guarantee when you are near the Amish, Sarah believes is that you will feel close to God.

Many years later she married Martin who is the love of her life and moved to England. There she started to write stories about the Amish. Recently after a lot of persuasion from her best friend she has decided to publish her stories. They draw on inspiration from her relationship with the Amish and with God and she hopes you enjoy reading them as much as she did writing them. Many of the stories are based on true events but names have been changed and even though they are authentic at times artistic license has been used.

Sarah likes her stories simple and to hold a message and they help bring her closer to her faith. She currently lives in Yorkshire, England with her husband Martin and seven very spoiled chickens.

She would love to meet you on Facebook at https://www.facebook.com/SarahMillerBooks

Sarah hopes her stories will both entertain and inspire and she wishes that you go with God.

Made in the USA
Coppell, TX
18 November 2020

41588634R00059